Skeleton
at School

Springy and Sam

Skeleton at School

Jan Needle

Illustrated by Kate Aldous

MAMMOTH

For
Tamineh and Danyal
and
Shireen and Jahan

First published in Great Britain 1988
by William Heinemann Ltd
Published 1990 by Mammoth
an imprint of Mandarin Paperbacks
Michelin House, 81 Fulham Road, London SW3 6RB

Mandarin is an imprint of the Octopus Publishing Group

Copyright © 1988 Jan Needle

ISBN 0 7497 0074 2

A CIP catalogue record for this title
is available from the British Library

Printed in Great Britain
by Cox & Wyman Ltd, Reading, Berkshire

Contents

1 · In At The Deep End

Starting at a new school can be pretty hard work. To start in the middle of a term, a week later than you're expected, can be awful.

Springy and Sam, over breakfast at The Kerry, had made it clear that they thought they were heroes – and deserved something for it.

'What about my dog?' said Springy. He went slightly red at the same time, because he knew he was trying it on. Dad put his head back and laughed.

'The only dog you'll see is a hot one,' he said. 'If the school dinners aren't boiled spuds and stodge like they were at my old school.'

'But it's not fair,' Springy went on. 'Me and Sam worked like mad last week getting this place fit. And we missed a week of school. We deserve a reward.'

Uncle Jock, the old fellow who lived in a secret

attic at the top of the boarding house, looked puzzled.

'Surely a week off school *is* a reward?' he said. 'School and me didn't agree one smidge.'

Sam, who had been keeping quiet to see how her brother got on, decided he needed help.

'No, honest, Dad,' she said. 'Springy's right. We *were* good, weren't we, Mum? And going in late's going to be horrible.'

Their mother, who was filling a thermos jug for Dad to take to work, nodded seriously.

'It probably will be,' she agreed. 'So you'd better not be any later, had you? Get your coats and go.'

'But Mum!' said Springy. '*Can* I have my dog this week? *Please*?'

'No,' said Mum. 'I never said you could have one. In fact, I said you *never* could! I've told you before and I'll tell you again. You're far too lazy.'

Mr Price watched his son's face begin to go funny, and took a hand. Actually, he put a hand under Springy's chin and lifted him by it until he was standing.

'You're a chancer,' he said. 'You can have a pet soon, as soon as we're settled in. But it will *not* be a dog. So think again.'

'How about a scorpion?' Sam suggested. 'Then you could put it in their bed for being so ungrateful.'

Springy, pulling himself angrily away from his father's touch, agreed.

The walk to Lapwing School was not long, but for a first time, it was exciting. They did not wear uniform – very few kids did – but it was easy to tell who was going, and there were plenty of them. It was for this reason they had not let their mother come with them.

'But you won't know where to go,' she'd said. 'You'll be terrified.'

'We've met Mrs Jackson,' Sam had snapped. 'We'll ask a kid where her classroom is. We're not babies, you know.'

Mrs Jackson had come to The Kerry the week before, to see why they had not turned up on their first Monday. She was very peculiar, for a teacher, full of funny sayings and jokes. She also seemed much more sensible than the average – she had told them to take the rest of the week off to help get the new house straight!

As they moved down the last broad, leafy road to the schoolyard, they began to recognise some of the other children. It was funny, Sam said, that although they'd never really spoken to anyone, they knew so many faces. One girl actually waved. Sam waved back.

'I saw her in the chippy,' she said. 'I think her father runs the pub.'

'Look,' said Springy. 'There's that horrible boy from the takeaway.'

'Yeah,' said Sam. 'He spat at me on Thursday. I'll batter him if I get the chance.'

The boy was running, whooping as he went. As he passed smaller girls he pushed and shoved at them.

'Pig,' said Sam. 'Just let him try anything on with me.'

They looked round at the sound of clattering feet, to see another boy, bigger than the first, racing after them. The twins recognised *him*, as well.

'They must be mates,' said Springy. 'They're always in the takeaway, playing the machines. I wonder what they're called.'

In the playground, they looked around for somebody to ask the way to Mrs Jackson's class. It wasn't as easy as they'd hoped. The kids were screaming about like meteors, rocketing into groups and bouncing off the walls. It was like a giant game of tag.

'A madhouse,' said Springy. 'I thought our last place was noisy, but this is ten times worse. It's as if we were invisible.'

But they weren't. After a couple of minutes – which seemed much longer – the pub girl came up to them. She was with a friend.

'Hallo,' she said. 'You're new, aren't you? I'm Jenni, and this is Joanna. We're in Mrs Jackson's.'

Springy and Sam beamed.

'Great!' said Sam. 'So are we! I'm Sam, and this is Springy. We're twins, but you'd never know it, and he's called that because he's idle. His real name's Stephen.'

'Hers is Samantha,' said Springy. 'But only people who hate us call us that. Like our Mum and Dad when they're furious.'

The girls laughed, and they chatted for a while. Jenni and Joanna said the school was all right, and the teachers were all right – except Mrs Jackson, who was mad – and most of the kids were all right.

'What?' asked Springy. 'Even them two?'

He pointed at the boys from the takeaway, who were still zooming about knocking people over. The two girls made faces.

'Ergh!' said Jenni. 'Alker and Beavham. Ooh no, they're horrible. They bully and kick and they're always getting people into trouble. My Dad says they should have drowned them at birth!'

'My Dad said they did drown Beavham, but they stopped just too soon,' said Joanna. 'He's weird. He's a psychowhatsit. A nutter.'

'Ooh look,' said Jenni. 'There's Cath. She owes me twelve pence. Are you coming?'

Sam shook her head.

'Where's the classroom?' she said. 'Mrs Jackson's. Mum gave us a note and I don't want the class to see. I'll put it on her desk.'

'She might be there,' said Joanna. 'She comes in early. It's through them doors and two down on the left. Class K. There's a green dinosaur on the door. Springy? You coming over?'

Springy blushed. He didn't want to be seen alone with *three* strange girls on his first day!

'Where's the Boys?' he said. 'I drank too much tea this morning!'

In the classroom, Sam felt very happy. It was huge, compared with their last school, huge and light and pleasant. The walls were covered in pictures and posters and coloured diagrams. When she stood still, and listened, she could hear water.

Water? She cocked her head. Yes, running water. She followed the sound, puzzled and excited. Until she came to the corner, and found the pond.

It was marvellous. It was almost as big as a single bed, and you had to climb steps up to it. The water was clear, and green, and lovely, full of weeds and bubbles. At one corner was a small waterfall of stones, with pumped water splashing and bubbling down it.

There were dark shapes in the depths! Fish!

Small shoals of darting ones, and bigger, slower, secret ones. It was absolutely perfect.

Sam put her bag on the table beside the pool, the table which held jars of fishfood and clean sand and so on. She realised that her mouth was slightly open. Just like a fish herself. She laughed, and shut it.

'What you laughing at?' said a voice behind her. It was a nasty voice, a boy's voice, a sneery voice. She knew before she turned that it would be Alker or his mate.

It was Alker. He had blondish hair and a pale, freckly face. His mouth was curled.

'Mind your own business,' said Sam. 'I was looking at the pond.'

'Biology pool,' said Alker. 'You could drown in that, you know. It's deep.'

'You'd have to be thick to fall in, wouldn't you?' said Sam. 'Have you been in, Alker?'

He was surprised that she knew his name. Also that she did not seem afraid of him. He moved forward, as if he was going to give her a shove.

Sam made a fist.

'Watch it, you,' she said. 'Or I'll smash your teeth. I don't like spitting bullies.'

Alker changed his face. It went from being curled and sneery and nasty, to the sunniest of smiles. Sam was amazed. He looked really nice. It was a big, wide, friendly, jolly smile.

Then Alker leaned forward and caught the end of her bag. Very gently, he pushed it. Very gently, it pushed the jars of fishfood, and the box of sand, across the polished table.

'Hey!' squeaked Sam.

But it was too late. With three separate and quite big splashes the jars and boxes fell into the water. Sam leaped then, and grabbed her bag. Alker moved backwards, still smiling.

That was when the door opened, just as Sam was opening her mouth to let fly.

Mrs Jackson walked in.

2 · Rogues' Gallery

The week before, when they had met her at The Kerry, Springy and Sam had decided Mrs Jackson was weird. Then, in the playground, Jenni and Joanna had said she was mad. Now Sam began to see the madness at work.

Mrs Jackson had an odd face, long like a fiddle, with big bushy eyebrows. Her mouth was never still. She made a funny tutting noise as she walked towards the biology pool.

'Peter Alker,' she said. 'Where you are there's trouble. And you, the new girl. What is it today, nice Sam or naughty Samantha?'

Peter Alker put on a smile even more dazzling than the one he'd used before tipping the stuff into the pool.

'I don't think she did it on purpose, Mrs Jackson,' he said. 'I think it was an accident.'

Sam was astonished. The little liar!

'It wasn't an accident!' she squeaked. 'He did it on purpose!'

'Gloriana Muffins,' said Mrs Jackson. 'A mystery. Well well, I like a bit of detective work to get the morning going.'

She did not seem angry, just interested. Nor did she appear to notice the strange thing she'd just said. Gloriana Muffins!

'It's not a mystery,' said Alker. 'This new girl was looking at the pond and I walked up behind her. I spoke and I think she was surprised. She grabbed her bag and the stuff got pushed in.'

'Liar!' hissed Sam. 'You're a rotten liar, Alker.'

Mrs Jackson smiled. Her mouth was rubbery, like a TV comedian's.

'Oh, I see you've been introduced,' she said. 'How nice. By the way, pass me the fish net, Peter. We'd better get the stuff out, hadn't we?'

She laughed.

'Maybe the fish will eat and eat until they get like Jaws! Maybe they'll burst the tank and eat the children! Maybe they'll take over the world!'

'It wasn't an accident,' Sam repeated. 'I threatened to thump him and he pushed my bag to make the stuff fall in.'

Mrs Jackson, unlike any teacher Sam had ever seen, was lying full-length on the platform by the pond, dibbling in the water with a long-handled net. She was grunting.

'You were going to thump him, were you? How unladylike.'

Alker snorted.

'Stupid,' he said. 'No girl would dare to thump me. She's making it up, Miss.'

Mrs Jackson twitched her eyebrows.

'If your mother had thumped you more when you were littler,' she said, 'she might have had a human being on her hands. Instead of a savage.'

Sam goggled. Could a teacher say that? A dripping can of fish food was thrust at her.

'There you are. Check that no water's gone in, will you? Otherwise the whole class will be on dry bread for a week, to pay for more.'

'I won't,' said Alker. 'Because it was nothing to do with me. I'm not going to suffer because some stupid girl can't control her schoolbag.'

Mrs Jackson, red-faced and puffing, got up. She had the rest of the stuff.

'Quite right,' she told the boy. 'Justice and fairness in everything. In fact, you've been such a good lad, Peter, you can go to the Head's garden and feed Cherry and Pip. One handful from each of the three sacks. No more.'

With his lovely smile, Alker left the room. Sam, miserable and furious, faced the teacher.

'It wasn't me,' she said. 'I was standing looking in. He's a bully. He spat at me last week. I hate him.'

'Holy chimps,' said Mrs Jackson. 'Don't sound so sad about it. Last time we met, you had a foul temper. Why aren't you dancing about with rage?'

Sam did not know what to say. This woman was *definitely* loony. She was suddenly taken by the shoulder, and pushed smartly across the room. Mrs Jackson stopped her in front of a long green wallboard. She pointed at the painted words above it.

'Rogues' Gallery,' she said. 'Do you know what that means?'

Sam did not. Mrs Jackson opened up a nearby drawer. It was full of pictures. Kids' pictures, bright and splodgy. Each one had a name printed on it, in big white letters. She pulled out a face with yellow hair and brown lumps.

'Freckles,' she said. 'It's meant to be Peter Alker. What does it say?'

Sam read off the words. Perilous Pete.

'Perilous,' said Mrs Jackson. 'It means dangerous. That's Peter Alker for you. Dangerous.'

She flipped out another picture. This one was marked Bad Bill.

'That's his friend,' she said. 'Bad Bill Beavham. You'll have a lot of trouble with them. You have been warned.'

Mrs Jackson slammed the drawer shut and grinned.

'Every time anyone's bad,' she said, 'their picture goes up in the Rogues' Gallery for a week. You have to paint it yourself, and do the lettering, and you lose class points.' She waved towards a wall chart. 'Stars,' she said. 'For treats and outings.'

Sam nodded.

'Is he going up this week? For the fish thing?'

'Ah,' said Mrs Jackson. 'But I have no *proof*, have I? It's his word against yours. I have no real evidence. Only *circumstantial*.'

Sam felt herself going red. She thought she might explode.

'Ah, that's better. A sign of the red-haired tantrum! But hold it in, Sam, it will do you good.'

Sam swallowed. She gritted her teeth. She breathed deeply. The temper went away. Mrs Jackson patted her on the shoulder.

'Good,' she said. 'We have to be fair in this classroom, child. It's the only way. So if I put Peter in the Rogues' Gallery, I'd have to put you up too. And that would *not* be good, would it? Not on your very first day?'

The door burst open then and the kids flooded in. Sam had no time to reply, or think. Mrs

Jackson, with a final pat, turned towards her desk. The row the children made did not worry her. She was surrounded by chaos. She sat down at her desk until it died away. Then she began.

'Kids,' she said. 'The missing twins are here at last. Their names are Springy and Sam, and they are standing there like a pair of lemons. Damon, squeeze up and let Springy in. Good. Jenni, I can see the look in your eye. You can have Sam. Now – enough of this unbridled caperation. To work, to work!'

She was potty, she was nutty, she was mad. In break, Sam and Springy, in between making new friends, agreed on it. She shouted and raved, she swore at kids, she pretended to tear their heads off and kick them around the room. Springy thought she was brilliant. But Sam was not so sure.

'She didn't back me up,' she said. 'It's his smile, I reckon. He's a blue-eyed boy.'

'Rubbish,' said Springy. 'She's dead fair. Everyone says so.'

Sam was not convinced.

In the afternoon, they did biology. They talked about bones. Sam, remembering their Uncle Arthur, told the class how a wrist looked with a Collet's fracture. All bent into an S-shape, enough to make you throw up. Uncle Arthur had done his wrist three times. He was a fool.

Springy remembered something even better.

'We've got a skeleton,' he said. 'A real one. It's only got one leg.'

The class were split down the middle. Half of them believed him, half of them did not. Several hopped about, shouting 'Argh, Jim lad!' Others pretended to faint. When the fun was over, Mrs Jackson drew one on the board, and named some of the biggest bones.

But when the bell went, and everyone was racing out, she called Springy and Sam to her desk.

'Have you *really* got a skeleton?' she asked. 'I mean, a real one? No messing about?'

Sam was ready to lose her temper again. Didn't this woman believe *anything* they told her?

'Of course we have,' she snapped. 'We're not liars!'

'Ooh,' said Mrs Jackson. 'Harsh words, child.'

'Yes,' said Springy, cautiously. 'It's not exactly – '

Sam did not give him the chance to finish. He had been going to explain that it belonged to Uncle Jock.

She interrupted. 'It's got one leg and it lives in the attic. Do you think we made it up?!'

'It's a strange tale if you did,' smiled Mrs Jackson. 'But calm down, Sam, calm down.'

'Well,' said Sam.

'Oh dry up,' said Springy. 'Why did you ask, Miss?'

'It would be very useful to show the class,' she said. 'Wouldn't it just? I suppose there's no chance of you bringing it in, is there?'

Sam nodded vigorously.

'Of course there is,' she said. 'That would *prove* it, wouldn't it?'

'But we'd have to ask,' said Springy.

'Ah,' said Mrs Jackson.

3 · The Key to Everything

That 'Ah' from the teacher made Sam spit blood as they walked home a few minutes later.

'She didn't believe us,' she said. 'She never believes us. She'd rather believe that pig Peter Alker.'

'Oh shut up, Sam,' said Springy. 'You're talking codswallop. She only said "Ah"!'

'Yeah,' said Sam. 'Because you said we'd have to ask.'

'Well, we will. It's Uncle Jock's skeleton, not ours. We can't just take it, can we?'

'All right. But she thought you were just setting up an excuse for the morning, didn't she? So that you could come in and say, "Sorry, but Uncle Jock said no". That's what that "Ah" meant, isn't it?'

How should I know, thought Springy. The only thing he was fed up about was being kept behind by the questions. He'd wanted to go on making mates. But now the roads outside the school were almost empty.

'I told you Jenni was nice, didn't I?' Sam said. 'Joanna as well. What's that kid you were sat next to like? What's he called?'

'Damon,' replied Springy. 'He's a bit slow, I think. You know.'

'Slow?'

'Well – I think he's sort of . . . backward. He seems nice, but he didn't have his coat done up right. He's cack-handed.'

Sam saw this as another part of Mrs Jackson's plot.

'See!' she said. 'She doesn't like us! She accused me of murdering her fish, and she thinks you're stupid! She's put you next to the school thicko!'

Springy didn't like this kind of talk. His best friend at their last school had had a crippled leg. Everyone had laughed at him, and called him Spider because of the way he walked.

'He's not the school thicko,' he said. 'He's all right. Anyway, he couldn't be stupider than you, could he?'

The first sound that they heard when they opened the front door to The Kerry was the vacuum cleaner. They ran into the middle room, their quarrel forgotten.

'Hello, Mrs Bagshaw!' yelled Springy, above the noise. 'Where's Trannie?'

The tubby cleaning lady clicked the hoover off with her foot.

'Hello, you two. He's upstairs, I think. He doesn't like the vacuum. Competition.'

She pulled her head back and shouted: 'Trannie! Pretty boy! Come to Mummy!'

Trannie was the best-trained budgie they had ever seen. Five seconds later there was a fluttering in the hall, and a chirrup. The small green bundle shot into the room and perched on Mrs Bagshaw's head.

'Sweenie!' it screeched. 'It's family care line time! How's your Dylan?'

'It's funny,' said Mrs Bagshaw. 'My Ernie

always listens to the BBC. But Trannie only picks up Picadilly. It must be his aerial!'

'Is Uncle Jock in?' asked Springy.

'Your mother is,' said a voice from the doorway. 'That's what I like about you two. Loyalty. It's Mrs Bagshaw and Trannie first, then Uncle Jock. Don't I even get a second thought?'

It was Mrs Price. Springy and Sam smiled. They knew she didn't mind.

'Hi, Mum. We've got to talk to him. For school.'

She came into the room.

'School,' she said. 'Yes, you've been, remember? It was your first day, remember? What was it like? Aren't you going to tell me?'

The children talked about school for twenty seconds. (It was 'all right'.) Then they wanted to race upstairs to Uncle Jock's little attic. But mother was not having any of it.

'Later,' she said. 'I need some shopping. Your Dad will be home quite early tonight for once, so we're going to have a proper meal. I've made a list out. It'll be a two bag each job.'

It wasn't until more than an hour later that they climbed the thirty-four stairs to the top attic, tired and sweaty from their chores. They stopped outside the little green and yellow door and listened.

'Maybe he's asleep,' said Springy. 'Is that snoring?'

There *was* a noise something like a snore, but not so regular.

'He's gone bionic. That sounds like metal to me. Iron or something.'

Springy knocked. The strange noise stopped. He knocked again.

'If it's the tax inspector, go away. If it's anybody else – you're welcome. Open up the door and stop wasting time.'

Inside, Uncle Jock was sitting at his tiny workbench. He beamed.

'Well, well. So you weren't eaten by wild teachers or the school cat. How did it go?'

'Great!' said Springy. 'We told them about the skeleton. And, and, and – '

'Can we *borrow* him?' asked Sam. 'Can Ahab go to school? That would be *brilliant*!'

'What was that funny noise, by the way?' said Springy. His sister snorted.

'Never *mind* that,' she said. '*Can* we, Uncle Jock? It would make their eyes pop out! And Miss Jackson's. I don't think she believed we'd *got* a skeleton.'

'*We* haven't,' said Springy. 'Uncle Jock has. *Please*, Uncle Jock. *Can* we?'

'One, two, three,' said Uncle Jock – to keep

them in suspense. 'No problem. Any time you like. Yes.'

The kids were wild with delight.

'Yippee!' yelled Sam. 'Yippee, yippoh, yippoo! Hey, you're *great*, do you know that?'

He smiled.

'I haven't got a car though, have I? How will Captain Ahab get there? He may only have one leg, but he can't hop.'

'Oh,' said Springy. 'She'll work that out. We'll ask her tomorrow. She's got a car.'

Uncle Jock remembered something. He picked up a file and a piece of metal.

'That's what I was doing when you knocked,' he told Springy. 'I was filing a skeleton key. Funny, eh? And now you want a skeleton.'

'A skeleton key?' said Springy. 'What, you mean a key shaped like a skeleton?'

'No no, it's just a name for a key that opens lots of locks, I don't know why. Your mother needs a key for the garden shed, and the cellar. This'll do both.'

The key was not cut like an ordinary one. It was just a thin T-shape on a longish shaft.

'Why would that open anything?' said Sam. 'It looks too skinny.'

'Exactly,' said Uncle Jock. 'You can wiggle it about inside the lock, until you find the right

levers to press. Hang on and I'll show you.'

He filed away for about three minutes. Then he held the key up, blew the metal dust off, and nodded.

'That was the snoring noise,' said Springy. 'The file. I said it was metal, didn't I?'

They all went outside. Uncle Jock locked his door with the proper key, then inserted the skeleton key into the hole.

It took him half a minute of jiggling and wiggling. And a little swear or two. Then the lock clicked, and the door creaked open.

He gave the key to Springy.

'That'll do the others,' he said. 'Tell your Mum to hang it on the kitchen door or something, so it doesn't get lost. What time's tea tonight?'

'When Dad comes home,' said Sam. 'He won't be late, Mum says. We'll call.'

Springy was looking at the key.

'That's *fantastic*,' he breathed.

They took it down to Mum.

4 · Duffing Up Damon

Springy and Sam bounced off to school next morning early, and in very good spirits. Dad was at home yet again, their mother had had a letter from someone who wanted to rent a room at The Kerry for a good long time, and they had the news of the skeleton to give to Mrs Jackson.

'We ought to make it look even *more* like a sailor,' said Springy. 'I expect Uncle Jock's got something. I know he's got a telescope to go under its arm.'

'Hey, maybe we could get a crutch from the hospital down the road!' added Sam. 'We could pin his trouser leg up and prop it under his armpit. That'd be good.'

Springy said, 'It's a pity Trannie's only a budgie. If he was a parrot we could have him sitting on Captain Ahab's shoulder saying "Pieces of Eight!"'

His sister punched him in the chest for being a fool.

'He wouldn't though, would he? He'd say "I've been up the creek with Umberto", or something equally ridiculous. We'd get expelled.'

'Yeah,' said Springy. 'It's a funny bird, isn't it? I wonder who Umberto is?'

They carried on in silence for a while, until they joined the main road that led to Lapwing School. There were not so many kids about, as they were early, but they recognised one or two.

'Hey,' said Sam. 'Isn't that your dimbo mate up there? Damon?'

Springy gave her a dirty look for being nasty, and followed her pointing finger.

'Yes,' he said. 'I wonder who he's looking for?'

Damon was walking along like a spy or a detective might. Sort of shifty, and looking over his shoulder and down alleyways between the shops.

'He's like a tramp,' said Sam. 'I wonder if he hasn't learnt to dress himself yet?'

'Oh give over, you,' said Springy. 'Uncle Jock looks like a tramp an'all, but you don't go on about him all the time, do you? He's great.'

'Ah,' said Sam. 'But he's been around. He's – Hey! Hang on! What's going off?'

Suddenly, as he was passing a little entry, Damon had jumped, as if he'd been stung, or hit

by a stone or something. He looked sideways, yelled, then darted off.

'Someone's after him!' said Springy. 'Someone's hiding down that ginnel!'

They did not have to wait very long for the next piece of excitement. As Damon pelted off through the early shoppers, two more boys appeared from down the alley. They were yelling.

'Damon! Damon! Dimmy-dimmy Damon!'

It was Peter Alker and Billy Beavham.

'Here, come back, Dimmy! We want to talk to you!'

Springy and Sam looked at each other.

'I sit next to him,' said Springy. 'I'm going after!'

'Brother,' said Sam. 'I'm right behind you!'

In fact, within ten seconds she was in front, because Springy had run into an old lady and had to apologise. He put on his best speed afterwards, but he could not quite catch up.

'Where did they go?' he panted. 'Silly old dame back there! She nearly broke my leg with her walking stick!'

'They've gone behind the school,' said Sam. 'I think they took that pathway there. Oh, I wish we knew the place better.'

They dashed down the lane, then turned left by a row of small locked garages. A long cobbled pathway, then the school appeared once more to their left. It was railed off, but they could see a gateway in the fence.

They pelted on, until they came to a dark yard behind the old part of the school, the part that was no longer used. It had a mass of cracked tar and concrete underfoot, and lots of blocked-off stairways.

After a few more steps, they stopped. Their blood was racing.

'We've lost them,' said Sam. 'Poor Damon's going to get a battering, I reckon.'

They heard a cry, quite near.

'No! Get off me! Leave me be!'

'Over there!' said Sam. 'Quick. Behind that shed affair!'

They clattered around, then stopped. In front of them, not far away, Alker and Beavham had got their prey captured. He was in a corner, facing them. As the twins watched, Beavham aimed a kick, which Damon tried to fend off with his wrist.

'Leave me alone! Leave me alone! Ow! Ow!'

Without another word, Springy and Sam raced in. Beavham turned, hearing their footsteps, and shouted to warn Alker.

Too late. Springy, in front by a fraction of a moment, piled into Alker. Beavham and Sam met head on, and Damon jumped on Beavham's back. Within a second, all five of them were on the floor, punching, clawing and kicking.

In another second, or maybe five, it was over. There was the thundering of bigger feet, and the thunderous roar of a teacher shouting. A man teacher, and very big. He picked them up like small, light parcels, and plonked them down on their heels, in separate places.

'Which class?' he roared. 'I know Alker and Beavham and you, boy. You're Class K. Mrs Jackson's lot. And what about you two?'

The twins nodded. Sam dabbed at her nose, which was bleeding slightly.

'Horrid children,' he said. 'I'll make sure she deals with you severely. Come on. March!'

'Hallo, Eric,' said Mrs Jackson, when he led them into the classroom. 'What have we here?'

Although Springy and Sam had been early, they were now only just on time. Most of the other kids were jostling to their places. Jenni and Joanna waved to Sam, enjoying the fun.

'Bad hats, I'm afraid,' said the big teacher. 'They were fighting round the back of the old school. I don't know who this pair are, but they say they're yours.'

Mrs Jackson nodded.

'Yes,' she said. 'Stephen and Samantha. They seem determined to get into the Rogues' Gallery.'

'It wasn't us!' said Sam. 'Alker and Beavham were duffing Damon up. We went to rescue him.'

'Liar!' shouted Alker. 'They started it, didn't they, Bill?'

'Shut up,' said the big teacher. 'It looked like a general free-for-all to me.'

'Yes,' said Mrs Jackson. 'That's always the problem, isn't it, Samantha? Lack of evidence. Thank you, Eric.'

The big teacher smiled and left. But Sam almost spat with rage at Mrs Jackson.

'You're not going to let them off *again*, are you?' she demanded. 'That's *ridiculous*!'

Mrs Jackson raised her eyebrows.

'I'll have to let you *all* off, won't I, child? You don't get into the Rogues' Gallery without evidence, do you? I don't believe in unfair punishments. Now – go and sit down. All of you.'

Jenni whispered noisily to Sam, 'She's trying to keep Alker and Beavham off the wall for a whole week. To see if it's possible. She's barmy.'

'Any more whispering, and innocent blood will flow!' shouted Mrs Jackson.

'See?' whispered Joanna. 'Nuts!'

At dinnertime, when her temper was better, Sam agreed to go with Springy to speak to Mrs Jackson. She was marking books at her desk, and looked up when they coughed.

'Oh hello,' she said. 'The Terrible Twins. Don't you want your lunch?'

'It's about the skeleton, Miss,' said Springy.

'Ah,' said Mrs Jackson. Just like the night before. 'There's a problem, I suppose.'

'No!' said Sam. 'Of *course* there's not! But we need some transport, don't we? When can you come and collect it?'

A big smile swept Mrs Jackson's funny, long face.

'Well I'll be cornswoggled,' she said. 'There *is* a skeleton! I was beginning to wonder if you might not just have made it up, or dreamed it!'

'Hah!' said Sam, hotly. 'Just like the biology pool! Just like the fight with those two bullies. You think we're liars, don't you?'

Springy was horrified. You couldn't talk to a teacher like that! But Mrs Jackson just smiled on, although it was a different type of smile.

'Sam,' she said. 'I work in proof. I will not punish people without evidence. You must like it or lump it in my class. Now – to more serious things. When can I get the skeleton? I can hardly wait.'

Sam did not speak. So Springy said, 'How about after school tomorrow? Will that do?'

'That will do nicely, thank you,' said Mrs Jackson, laughing to herself. 'It'll mean five stars for you, also. *Each.*'

Even Sam thought, Crikey . . .

5 · Disaster

There was a lot of excitement in The Kerry next morning – but it was nothing to do with Springy and Sam or the Skeleton Project.

When they got downstairs, breakfast was not on the table, and Mum was bouncing up and down like a two-year-old. Dad was perched on a stool by the sink with a mug of tea in his hand, grinning.

'Where's my cornflakes?' said Springy. He liked to be fed at the right time in the morning, and was miffed.

'Oh, get them yourself!' said Mum. 'I'm all at sixes and sevens today.'

'Get them myself! But I don't even know where they are!'

'Go hungry, then. How old are you? It's disgusting.'

Sam said, 'They're in that cupboard, beside the cooker. And before you ask me – no, I will *not* get them for you!'

It was all sorted out soon enough, and everyone had some kind of breakfast. But even Springy's need to get his face filled was almost forgotten because of his mother's antics.

'Come on,' said Sam. 'Spit it out, Mum. What's the big event?'

'It's our first lodger,' replied Mum. 'That young chap I told you about. He phoned again last night and he's coming today. He's agreed a *whopping* rate for the three months!'

'Three *months*!' said Springy. 'Blimey, why doesn't he just join the family?'

'That's why it's so good,' said Dad. 'The money will be coming in week by week, regular as clockwork, and your mother won't have to worry. He works for a big international computer firm, so he'll be nice and quiet, and he does long hours so he won't be under our feet all the time.'

Springy laughed.

'He sounds too good to be true,' he said. 'Are you sure you haven't dreamed him?'

Mum grinned as well.

'It is a bit like that, isn't it?' she agreed. 'He'll probably have an awful habit, like playing the trombone all night or something! Anyway – he's the first, and I'm looking forward to it.'

Sam got quite indignant.

'What about Uncle Jock?' she demanded. 'He was the first. Don't be so rotten.'

'He may have been the first, but the money we charge him won't pay off the mortgage,' said Dad. 'Or the bills. You've no idea how much keeping a place like this costs. It's horrendous.'

'But he did *help*,' said Sam. 'He's worth his weight in gold. Mum said so.'

'Oh yes, no sweat, I'm not complaining. But a *real* lodger, paying *real* money, is just what the doctor ordered. It couldn't have come at a better time, I'm telling you.'

The kids agreed, as they went to Lapwing, that it was a good job Uncle Jock hadn't turned up in the breakfast room to hear the conversation. He might have been upset.

'Anyway,' said Springy. 'I bet this new bloke's

not half as interesting. Although it will be fun to have someone new. And he knows about computers. Ace.'

'Boring,' said Sam. 'Anyway, you haven't even unpacked yours since we moved. I thought you'd grown out of it!'

Springy aimed a kick at her.

'You're just jealous because you can't even understand the games,' he said. 'I might be a computer wizard when I grow up.'

'Or a dustman!'

Further along the road they met Jenni and Joanna, which brought even more excitement. The night before, there had been a fight outside the pub. A big one.

'It was fantastic,' said Jenni. 'I should have been asleep because it was after closing time, but I was playing with Barbie and Ken under the bedclothes. Then the din got terrific. Joanna heard it right across the street.'

'Yeah,' said Joanna. 'My Mum's shop's about a hundred metres away, but when I looked out, there were fellers running all over, chucking bottles. Magic!'

The police had come, with sirens wailing, and six people had been carted off in a Black Maria. Jenni and Joanna had both been awake till after midnight.

'Crikey,' said Springy. 'Our Dad said it was a dead quiet pub, yours. He said you could take your granny there.'

'You usually can,' laughed Jenni. 'But it was a special football club do. There's two teams round here and they usually end up fighting. It's worst when they have a friendly.'

School, after all the buzz and jollity, seemed a little boring. Even Mrs Jackson, who could make most lessons interesting, was not at her best. She announced after the register that they were going to do music today. Modern music.

'That sounds all right,' whispered Sam to Joanna. 'Does she mean groups?'

'Does she heck,' whispered Joanna, making a face. 'She means playing metal pipes and bathtubs and that. She's got a bee in her bonnet.'

Mrs Jackson had, it turned out. She set up her equipment, and leered at them.

'Come on, you horrible lot,' she said. 'Shut the row up for a minute. I'm going to force some culture into your earholes. We're going to start off with *The Rite of Spring*, by Stravinsky.'

To Sam, the name meant nothing. But from the groan that went up all round the room, the other kids had heard it all before. Mrs Jackson banged her fist for silence, then put her finger on the button.

'You know the rules,' she said. 'There are stars to be won by people who can convince me they're really trying to understand this. But if I catch anyone messing about – it's the thumbscrews.'

The music started in reasonable silence from the class – and from Sam. She found it most peculiar, this piece – jangly, and surprising, and exciting in a funny way. It was certainly like nothing she'd ever heard before. She looked around to see how other people were reacting.

Boredom, pain, interest – and the naked desire of some to win stars. She almost giggled. And sadly, forgot to go on listening to the music.

After ten or fifteen minutes, the class had had enough. Mrs Jackson, who knew them like the back of her hand, switched off the tape recorder. She made a huge sweep with her hand.

'Now,' she said. 'Yell!'

For thirty seconds by the watch, she let them shriek and roar, to get it out of their systems. Then she shut them up.

'All right,' she said. 'That's enough music. But now we're going to go on talking about spring. How does that sound?'

'No!' shouted some of the kids. 'Not spring! Cars! Ships! Singers! Lady Di! Not spring!'

Mrs Jackson smiled. They quietened down again.

'Half an hour of spring,' she said. 'Then you can choose a topic. After all, that's what they pay me for, you know. To teach you things.'

After that, the day got pretty good – but Springy and Sam still found themselves anxious to get home. They'd arranged for Mrs Jackson to turn up at half past five, and they wanted to make sure that Captain Ahab was ready for her. They hardly said hello to Mrs Bagshaw as they flew past her, and they did not even go near the kitchen to see their Mum.

They raced it up the last flight to the secret attic, and Springy won by a short pant. He grabbed the handle and wrenched it round.

'Uncle Jock! We're ready!'

Sam, piling into the back of him, almost broke his wrist on the door.

'Come on, fool,' she said. 'What are you hanging about at? Get in there!'

Springy twisted the handle again. He jerked it noisily. He banged the door.

'It's locked,' he said. 'That's funny. There's no one in.'

His sister, naturally, thought he was potty, and had to try herself. When she was convinced, they trailed downstairs. They found their mother in the kitchen.

'Where's Uncle Jock?' asked Springy. 'We need him.'

Sam, looking at her mother's face, realised there was something wrong.

'Mum?' she said. 'What's wrong? Is something up?'

'Uncle Jock!' said Springy. 'He's not ... There's nothing ... ?'

Mrs Price looked tired and upset.

'He's not here,' she said. 'He's gone away. He went this morning.'

Springy grabbed her arm.

'Mum, is he ill or something? What's the matter?'

His mother shook her head.

'The matter is not to do with Uncle Jock,' she said. 'He's gone away, that's all. He's fine. The matter is to do with our new lodger. His firm rang up.'

'Oh cripes,' said Sam.

'Yes,' said Mrs Price. 'They've sent him to Holland on a rush job. He won't be coming after all.'

Springy said: 'But Uncle Jock – '

Sam dug him sharply in the ribs to shut his mouth.

He shut it.

6 · Facing Mrs Jackson

Mum was fed up. She was up to here with it. She was sick. She was so angry, that she didn't know what to do with herself.

She told them all this, at great length, as they hopped from one foot to the other trying to look interested.

The trouble was, that although she spelled out to them in words of one syllable what a disaster it was, and how they'd all end up in the poorhouse, and what a swine this feller was to let them down – the kids were desperate to get away.

They'd get no sense from Mum, clearly. So they wanted to go and speak to Mrs Hilda Bagshaw. Not only did she know everything, but she liked to talk about it. She'd tell them in a jiffy if there was any news of Uncle Jock. Or even if they'd ever see him again.

Springy, who was stupid about such things, would just have told his Mum to dry up and stop being boring, but luckily Sam knew better.

She put on a face that said 'Oh Mum, how sad', and asked her all the right questions. Consequently, if they'd listened, they'd have known everything there was to know about money, and debts, and mortgages, and running a boarding house. But they didn't listen.

Finally, they got away. As they dashed down the passage, Springy said: 'I could have murdered you in there! Why did you keep on and on? This is *serious*!'

'Oh, shut up,' said his sister. 'You're too dim to live, you are.'

They found the room that Mrs Bagshaw was in by following the sound of the vacuum cleaner. When she saw them in the doorway she beamed, and switched it off.

'Hello, you two,' she said. 'Come to see Trannie, have you? I wonder where he is.'

Before they could tell her not to bother, the tubby lady put two fingers in her mouth and did a loud and sharp whistle. From quite a distance away, in some other room, the whistle came back.

'Ten seconds,' she said. 'That's how long he'll be.'

'Mrs Bagshaw,' blurted Springy. 'Where's Uncle Jock? He's not upstairs. Mum says he's gone.'

The cleaning lady nodded.

'That he has,' she said. 'About ten o'clock this morning. He – Oh, here's my little bird.'

The small green budgie fluttered through the doorway. It perched on the handle of the upright vacuum cleaner and whistled.

'Sweenie! Sweenie! Meet him at the Picadilly disco, Friday night!'

'Rather them than me,' said Mrs Bagshaw. 'Hasn't he got an awful accent, that Mike Sweenie? Salford low, I call it.'

'Listen,' said Sam, quite rudely. 'Never mind Mike Sweenie for a minute. Will Uncle Jock be back tonight? It's *urgent*.'

Mrs Bagshaw chuckled.

'Tonight? I doubt it, love. Oh no, that's not very likely, not tonight.'

'But why?' said Springy. 'Where's he gone?

Mum says he's not ill.'

The tubby lady scratched her nose. She gave a little chirrup to her budgie, to keep it in the conversation, so to speak. The budgie nodded back at her.

'He's not, exactly. No, he's not ill. Although, come to that, some might think it was a disease. Mm.'

Even placid Springy was starting to get impatient.

'*What*?' he said. 'What's he got? Where's he gone?'

Mrs Bagshaw tutted.

'He never says,' she said. 'He just packs a plastic carrier bag and goes. I've never looked in it, like, but it don't look very full. I'd guess a pair of socks, a shirt and a clean pair of pants. I've never seen him with a handkerchief.'

'What?' said Sam. 'You mean he just . . . disappears?'

The budgie shrieked: 'Susie Mathis! Good afternoooon!'

'He does Susie Mathis terrific, doesn't he?' said Mrs Bagshaw fondly. 'Pity she's left.'

'Oh!' said Springy. 'Mrs *Bag*shaw!'

She patted him on the head.

'Sorry,' she said. 'Uncle Jock. Yes. Well, that's about it, really. All there is to know. He's a bit like your Dad when it comes to that. Now you see him – now you don't.'

'But Dad's a lorry driver. It's his job.'

Somehow, Mrs Bagshaw looked doubtful. Then she smiled.

'Mebbe,' she said. 'But it's just Uncle Jock's *way*. It was his job once, I suppose, him having been at sea all them years. He likes to wander. He's got wanderlust. Maybe he's got some aborigine blood, I dunno.'

'What do you mean?'

'Well, that's how they go on, isn't it? In Australia. Every now and then they just sort of go away into the Bush for a while.'

'Crikey,' said Springy. 'What for?'

Mrs Bagshaw made a funny face at him.

'How should I know? They call it going walkabout, that's all I know.'

'Nah,' said Springy. 'That's what the Queen does. And Princess Di.'

Sam was getting fed up.

'Look,' she said. 'When you've *quite* finished this fascinating conversation.'

'Sorry, love,' said Mrs Bagshaw. 'But there's nothing more I can tell you. Uncle Jock goes off sometimes. Whether he's an aborigine or not.'

'But – '

'And don't ask me how long, because I don't

know. *He* doesn't know. Nobody doesn't know. He'll just turn up one day, and say Hallo as plain as a pikestaff, and pay his back rent if he owes any. It's his way.'

Having polished off that subject, Mrs Bagshaw wanted to go on chatting, as it was very nearly time for her to go. But the twins did not want to talk to her. They needed to think. They made an excuse and left.

Up in the big bedroom that they were still sharing until The Kerry was properly sorted out, they *did* think. They racked their brains. After ten minutes they admitted it: they were stumped.

'What time is it?' said Sam. 'She'll be here soon, for the skeleton. What are we going to *do*?'

Springy glanced at his watch.

'Damn Uncle Jock,' he said. 'He's made us look proper fools, hasn't he? He *said* we could borrow Captain Ahab.'

'He could come back tomorrow,' said Sam, hopefully. 'He could even turn up tonight. Nobody *knows* he's gone walkabout.'

'Oh shut up, stupid. You're too old to believe in fairies. He's dropped us in it. *Right* in it.'

At twenty past five, the children went and stood out in the street. They could not bear the thought of their teacher speaking to their Mum.

'Mrs Jackson thinks we're liars already,' said Sam. 'If we let her in the kitchen Mum'll think it too. Oh why did Uncle Jock go like that?'

When she saw their glum faces, Mrs Jackson's face – which had been smiling through the windscreen at them – went thoughtful. She pulled the handbrake on and switched the engine off.

'Hello,' she said, winding down her window. 'Got a hitch, have we?'

The twins nodded. They did not want to speak.

'Never mind,' said Mrs Jackson, in a kindly voice. 'Plans never go quite right, do they? It was a nice idea.'

It was as plain as daylight that she did not believe a word they'd told her. She did not believe there was a skeleton at all. Both the twins were blushing red.

'It's not serious,' said Springy, lamely. 'Uncle Jock . . . well.'

'We'll get it,' said Sam. 'Honestly. We'll work something out.'

Mrs Jackson could see they were embarrassed, so she didn't use any funny words, or make faces. She just nodded.

'I'm sure you will,' she said.

They turned away as she started up her engine.

7 · The Secret Weapon

Even when their Dad came home from work Springy and Sam did not bother to ask if they could go into Uncle Jock's room. The answer would be no, and no arguments would ever change it.

In any case, Mum and Dad were too tied up in their own worries to care about the kids'. About the missing lodger, the unpaid bills, and what would happen next.

'It's been one disaster after another, this dump,' they heard Dad say. 'If it doesn't get better soon we'll have to sell the ruddy place.'

Normally, this would have terrified the twins, because they thought The Kerry was fantastic. Today, though, they had too much on their minds to care.

The worst thing, they both agreed, had been Mrs Jackson's face.

'She thinks we're rotten liars,' said Sam. 'She thinks we make up stories. It's horrible.'

'Yeah,' said Springy. 'And you know what she reckons about proof, and evidence. Until she *sees* Captain Ahab she'll *never* believe us.'

'Or anything else we say,' said Sam.

They were in the big bedroom, and they had had their tea. Soon it would be bedtime.

'I was really looking forward to tomorrow, too,' said Springy. 'I could just see the look on Alker's and Beavham's faces when they saw the bones. They didn't believe us, either. No one did.'

That, of course, was not true. At least half the class had believed them when they said they had a skeleton, and they'd told Jenni and Damon and Joanna lots more about it. Even they – their mates – would wonder now. If they were rotten liars . . .

It was all too much for Sam. She went and kicked her teddy bear. Hard.

'We'll have to break in in the dead of night,' she said. 'We'll have to smash the door down. If

we can't take Ahab, I'm not going into school.'

Springy, who was sitting on his bed, had his mouth open, looking soft. He'd just had an idea.

'Hey,' he said. 'You're a fool, aren't you? We're both fools. We don't *have* to break in, do we?'

Sam, feeling a bit ashamed, picked up the bear and hugged it better. She looked at her brother.

'What do you mean? It's locked. We tried it.'

Springy grinned.

'Yes. And what's downstairs, eh? On the kitchen door?'

She still looked blank. He gave her a clue.

'For skeletons?'

It sank in. Sam almost danced for glee.

'The key! The skeleton key! Springy, you're a genius!'

The feeling of happiness, that all their troubles were over, did not last long. Sam went to the bedroom door and listened. There was no sound down below.

'They're not watching telly,' she said glumly. 'They've got too much to talk about. They'll be sitting in the breakfast room, won't they?'

'Oh heck,' said Springy. 'They could talk for ages. They could go on all night.'

Sam went to the window, and pulled open the curtain. It was almost dark.

'There is another way to get the key,' she said. 'We don't *have* to go through the breakfast room to the kitchen, do we?'

Her brother joined her at the window. The lights in the tennis club were visible, across the darkened courts behind their garden.

'Is there?' he said. 'How?'

Sam's plan was simple, and it was quite daring. They would creep downstairs, she reckoned, and go out of the front door. Then they would creep round the side of The Kerry, open the back door, and take the key off its hook. Their parents, only a few metres away, would never know.

'They'll hear us,' said Springy. 'They'll lock the front door while we're in the garden. And the back. We'll be stuck outside all night.'

'You're chicken.'

'I'm sensible. It's ridiculous. A stupid plan.'

'Can you think of a better one?'

'No.'

They both laughed out loud. It was exciting. They could hardly wait.

They did wait, though, until it was quite a lot darker. They waited until after Mum had shouted upstairs to make sure they were in bed. Until they were sure she had gone back into the breakfast room to carry on talking to Dad.

'Come on,' said Springy, after listening at the landing for a while. 'The coast's clear. Don't forget the torch.'

The Kerry was quite an old house, built in 1902. Many of the floorboards creaked, as did the stairs. The journey to the front door was nerve-racking. They had to keep pausing while they held their breaths and listened. But at last they were out, with the door left on the latch so that they could get back in again.

'Should one of us stay on guard?' asked Springy. 'What if they *do* find it open and lock it? What if a thief comes along?'

'Shut up and shift,' said Sam. 'Speed's the thing. Stop mithering and move.'

Round in the back garden, they could not resist creeping up to the breakfast room window and peeping in. Because there were only tennis courts behind them, and no houses, their parents had not drawn the curtains. Mum was sitting at the table, leaning on one elbow, and Dad was in an easy chair, with his legs stretched out towards the gas fire.

'They don't *look* very worried,' said Sam, almost disappointed. 'The way they were going on earlier, you'd think the end of the world had come!'

'They look settled,' said Springy. 'Let's hurry

up before they change their minds.'

The twins dropped back from the window and went to the back door. It was unlocked. Half a minute later, they had the skeleton key, on the piece of string.

'Great,' said Sam. 'We're just like *real* burglars. They use skeleton keys.'

'Yes,' said Springy. 'But not many of them steal real skeletons!'

They scuttled back to the front door, almost forgetting to be quiet. But the light under the breakfast room door reminded them, and they put the catch on very gently. It would be disastrous to be found out now! Each board seemed to creak this time, each tread on the stairs appeared to be old, and loose, and noisy. When they were outside their bedroom once more, they stopped to get their breath.

'One more flight,' whispered Sam. 'Then the skeleton's ours. Fantastic.'

As they approached the little door, Springy had a sudden doubt.

'Sam,' he said. 'Do you think we ought to? We could get into terrific trouble.'

Sam pushed him in the back.

'Don't be stupid. He said we could take the thing, didn't he? Anyway, if you think we're going back now after coming all this way, you're nuts.'

'But what about putting the key back? And what about – '

Sam grabbed the torch and thrust the skeleton key into the lock. By luck, it turned first time, without any jiggling. The door opened.

'Too late,' she said. 'We've done it. We can't get any worse trouble than we've got already, can we? So let's get in. Here, grab the torch.'

Together, they walked into the room. In case anyone saw it, they did not use the light. Slowly, Springy flashed the thin beam of the torch around the cramped and crowded room. It looked very strange, and eerie, like in a ghost train tunnel.

'Ooh!' went Sam. 'Cripes, doesn't he look weird?'

Captain Ahab had appeared before them, white and glaring. He was grinning through his nasty, yellow teeth.

'Doesn't he look *big*?' said Springy. 'He must be six foot tall. Sam – he's all joined up with wires and things. He's enormous.'

He stopped. His sister said nothing, but they could both see what a problem they had on their hands.

'Wires,' said Sam at last. '*Now* what are we going to do?'

8 · Pandemonium

Although they didn't want to, both of them knew they would have to turn the light on after all. First, though, Springy flashed the torch onto his wrist. It was late.

'They'll be coming to bed soon,' he hissed. 'If they walk into the hall and see the light, we've had it.'

'We'll close the door,' said his sister. 'Quick – nip downstairs first and turn *our* light out. Otherwise Mum'll come up to tell us off.'

Springy did. Downstairs, there was still nothing to be heard. But Dad might have to get up very early, so they could not bank on safety for very long. His mouth was dry when he got back to the attic.

Close to, the skeleton of Captain Ahab was even spookier than it looked in the torchlight. Under its loose, dusty clothes, the bones were old, and yellow, and cracked, with stains on them that could easily have been blood.

'Didn't Uncle Jock say he was a sailor?' asked Sam. 'Maybe he was a pirate. Maybe he lost his leg in some terrible fight.'

'Can skeletons haunt you if you disturb them?' said Springy. He didn't like this lark very much. It was beyond a joke. 'Maybe we should leave him be.'

For a moment, Sam looked as if she might agree with him. Then she flicked Ahab's nose bone with her finger. It made a sharp click.

'He wouldn't dare,' she said. 'We'll boil him down for soap. He's only a collection of dead old bones.'

The real problem, however, was not fear, but just how they could handle the skeleton. He was joined together with twisted wire at every joint, and was kept upright by a long metal stand with a heavy round base.

Somehow, because he was so thin, they had thought he would be light. But, of course, he was not. The base itself had to be very heavy, just to stop him falling over.

Two attempts to lift him, and carry him as if he was still standing, just left them breathless.

'Take the head,' said Springy, after a breather. 'I'll take the feet. The foot. When I say so, we'll push him over so he's lying down.'

That was not a bad plan, except that when it

came to it, they realised it was impossible. Whichever way they tried to lie him, there was too much junk in the tiny room. They'd get him halfway down, then have to push him quickly upright before he crashed into something else.

After fifteen minutes' hard work, Captain Ahab was exactly as he had been when they came into the room. The children were sweaty and desperate.

'We've got to do *something*,' hissed Sam. 'We've been *ages*. They'll come up soon.'

At that exact moment – as if they'd been waiting for a cue – their parents made a noise downstairs. A door slammed. The children froze.

'That was the breakfast room,' Springy whispered. 'They're on their way to bed. We'd better be really quiet now.'

For perhaps two minutes, neither of them

moved. Sam almost giggled once, but she kept it in.

'What's up?' whispered Springy. 'Keep quiet.'

Then he noticed, too, that Sam was holding Ahab's hand. Ridiculous!

Two minutes isn't very long, but it feels like ages when you're trying to be still. Because they heard no more noises from below, the children did not wait forever.

'I've had an idea,' Springy announced. 'Let go his mitt and sneak over to that workbench there. See that pair of pliers? The ones with the red handles? They should do the trick.'

Sam, puzzled, did not argue. She did not even ask what her brother had in mind. Before very long, in fact, she knew. They had the knack, did the twins, of guessing what each other was thinking.

'Will it be enough?' she said. 'Won't they just laugh at us?'

'It'll be better than nothing, won't it? And they'd have to be pretty thick to find it funny!'

Because they were so late to bed in the end, the children overslept in the morning. When their mother noticed, and rushed upstairs to wake them, it took ages to get them going. Sam broke a pint of milk at the table, and they were halfway to the school before Springy remembered his bag. Lessons had already started before they stumbled into the classroom.

'Aha,' said Mrs Jackson, looking up. 'The wanderers return.'

She put on a tragic face, and spoke in a daft voice, like an actor.

'Alas, alas – McNab ye have not found! This is the end of all my hopes and dreams!'

'McNab?' said Sam. 'Who's McNab?'

Three idiots put their hands up, hoping to get stars: 'I know, Miss! I know! Oh Miss, Miss!'

Mrs Jackson laughed.

'You know in a pig's patootie,' she said. 'Only me and McNab know. He's a visitor I was expecting, and he didn't come. Now, S and S – sit down.'

Everyone was too used to Mrs Jackson to

worry much about the mystery visitor, and in any case, they were talking about sport, so most of the kids wanted to get back to the lesson. Springy and Sam, pleased not to have lost stars for being late, went to their places.

'Ooh,' said Jenni, to Sam. 'You look terrible! You've got all black rings under your eyes!'

'Yeah,' said Sam. 'I was up late. We didn't get to bed until – '

'Sam,' said Mrs Jackson. 'If you don't stop wittering, horrid child, I will sell you to a circus.'

'They wouldn't want her,' shouted Alker. 'Even the chimps would kick her out!'

At last the time for the biology lesson came round. The kids changed tables, and the specimens came out. Mrs Jackson, to everyone's surprise, started on about her visitor again.

'This McNab,' she said. 'He's a very useful man to have when you're doing biology, which is why I'm sorry he could not be here. I suspect the reason is that some children have stars in their eyes, rather than getting stars on the wall chart.'

With Springy, it clicked. He glanced across at Sam, and saw that she had worked it out as well. Mrs Jackson was talking about Ahab – and the fact that they had not brought him. What a rotten trick!

Mrs Jackson, watching them, smirked. Then,

sadly, she took the private joke too far.

'He comes from Bonnie Scotland, I believe, does Mr McNab,' she said. 'Or perhaps I should pronounce it in the old-fashioned way, as *boney* Scotland.'

Although Peter Alker was a bully and a pest, he was not thick. He latched onto the riddle instantly. He pointed at Springy, then Sam.

'She means that skeleton they made up!' he shouted. 'That's who McNab is! They said they had a skeleton and they haven't, have they? Now we know!'

Sam stood up, blazing mad.

'Well we have, so there!' she said. 'And he's not Scottish and he's not called McNab. He's Welsh and he's called Ahab!'

Beavham stood up and joined in.

'Yah,' he said. 'If you've got McNab, where is he, eh? You don't believe it, do you, Miss? They're liars, ain't they?'

'Ah,' said Mrs Jackson. 'Calm down, everyone. Alker, Beavham. Sit. And you, Sam.'

Sam was wild.

'They're right though, aren't they? You don't believe us, do you? You don't believe we've got a skeleton?'

The class became very quiet. Mrs Jackson's funny mouth made a very funny shape. She was on the spot.

'Well,' she said. 'You must admit . . . '

'Ooh!' went Sam. It was a noise of pure disgust. She looked across at her brother, who was already unzipping his bag.

'Springy!' she said. 'Show!'

Slowly, he pulled at something in the bag. Something in another bag, of see-through plastic. Kids all over the room stood up, and jostled, and craned their necks.

Springy jumped onto his seat so that everyone could see him.

'Meet Captain Ahab,' he said.

He held aloft the skull, dangling in the plastic, looking horrible.

There was pandemonium.

9 · Evidence!

It was difficult to tell who was doing what for real and who was just messing about.

Some of the girls began to shriek, and threw themselves full-length on the floor like fainting heroines in a Victorian-style TV drama series. Some of the boys held their stomachs and made disgusting vomiting noises. Others tried to knock Springy off his seat so that they could grab at the skull to see if it was real.

There was no doubt in Alker's mind.

'It's a fake!' he shouted. 'It's made of plastic! I've seen them in the joke shops in Tib Street!'

'You're stupid,' shrieked Sam. 'It is *not* a fake. We've got the rest of him at home.'

Beavham, who wanted to join in but could not think of anything sensible to say, yelled: 'Well it's a stupid name for a skeleton, anyway. McNab!'

'It's not McNab,' Springy shouted back. 'It's Ahab. It's Uncle Jock's.'

'Make up your mind,' bawled Alker. 'It can't have three names! Anyway, it's made of plastic!'

The noise was terrific, and the classroom was a sea of bodies, pushing, shoving, and jostling. Mrs Jackson shouted terrible threats, of hanging and flogging, before they all sat down. She mopped her brow.

'Well,' she said. 'What a performance. The next one to speak out of turn goes to the rack to be stretched and slimmed. Springy. Bring that disgusting morsel here.'

Springy walked out to the front with the skull. Sam, unasked, came out to join him. Mrs Jackson, not the slightest bit horrified, took out the skull and looked at it.

'Well, Alker,' she said. 'The joke's on you, I fear. It's real, all right. Now you two – what *is* it called? McNab, Ahab, or Uncle Jock?'

'It's Ahab,' said Springy.

'Ah,' said Mrs Jackson. 'Something to do with whales, was he?'

'That's right,' said Sam. 'He was born in Cardiff.'

Mrs Jackson laughed.

'I think that's a mistake,' she said. 'A different kind of Wales. It's a grown-up's joke.'

'But Uncle Jock – '

'Who *is* Uncle Jock?'

'It's his skeleton,' said Springy.

Peter Alker hooted.

'Did you dig him up, then?' he shouted. Everyone laughed. Sam turned on him.

'I'd like to bury *you*,' she snapped. 'You're jealous, that's all. You're like some other people who think we tell lies.'

Springy blushed, and looked at the teacher. She caught the look.

'Whoops!' she said. 'I'm being got at. Well, I must admit it, Sam. I did have me doubts.' She paused, and put on her 'silly joke coming' face. Everyone waited. 'I'll make no *bones* about it!'

The whole class groaned. Then the lesson began in earnest. The skull was passed round, and looked at, and explained, and sniffed, and poked, and even tasted by one bright spark. They had a lovely time. When the bell went, Miss Jackson announced five stars each for Springy and Sam, and almost everybody cheered. *Almost* everybody . . .

As they made to race out, having watched the teacher lock the skull away, the twins were called across to her table.

'I'd like a chat with you,' she said. 'Are you busy?'

'We are,' said Sam. 'We've got to get home. It's important.'

'It's a plan – ' said Springy, but a dirty look from his sister shut him up.

'Oh,' said Mrs Jackson. 'Never mind. How about just before afternoon lessons, then? Will you be back on time, or are you planning on being late twice today?'

'That's all right,' said Sam. 'See you.'

At home – where they conned Mum into thinking they'd forgotten something – they made sure the coast was clear before sneaking up to Uncle Jock's attic. Springy bent the carpet back outside his room, to reveal the skeleton key underneath.

'She didn't mention it,' he said. 'It's a good job she didn't need it to open up the shed.'

'I'll keep guard,' said Sam. 'Shut up talking and get the stuff.'

Springy went to work with the pliers, and less than five minutes later he rejoined his sister outside the door. He held up the bag, then locked the door.

'Both hands and his foot,' he said. 'We might get five more stars.'

'What about the key?'

'Same place. We'll get a leg or something for tomorrow. We'll show 'em!'

Up the stairs, their mother shouted, 'Would you like a cup of tea?' Then stood back as they thundered past her, on their way back to school.

'Oh well,' she said. 'It was just a thought.'

It was a bit harder avoiding their classmates, but Springy and Sam managed to get into the room alone. They stood by the teacher's desk, pleased with themselves.

'Where shall we put them?' said Sam. 'Why don't we arrange the hands round the register? She might have a heart attack!'

'We could borrow someone's gym shoe for his toes,' added Springy. 'Who's got the biggest feet?'

That was Beavham. But while they were searching round his table for a shoe, his friend Alker walked through the door.

'Oy, oy,' he said. 'Mrs Jackson's blue eyed beauties. What are you doing? Nicking something?'

Before they could answer, Alker had walked up to the teacher's table. He spotted the hands and foot of the skeleton.

'Yuck,' he said. 'Filthy!'

'Leave them alone,' said Sam. 'You'll break them!'

Both she and Springy launched themselves towards the table to stop him.

But they were too late. He grabbed a long, boney hand and held it above his head.

'It's not yours anyway,' he said. 'It's your Uncle Jock's. I bet you didn't even ask him, did you?'

Springy and Sam were close. Every time they tried a snatch, though, Alker hopped backwards. He was grinning, happy that he'd made them mad.

'What would you do if I chucked it out the window?' he said. 'There's plenty of dogs round here. I bet they'd eat it quick enough.'

He dodged round Sam and headed for the biology pool, on its raised platform. He bounced up the stairs to the window just behind it. Holding the bones above his head, he fiddled with the catch, as the twins tried to reach and grab.

'Get down, Bonzo,' he said to Springy. 'Don't be such a greedy dog!'

'Give it *here*!' said Sam. 'If you break it, Alker, I'll *murder* you!'

Alker did. Trying to get both hands to the window catch at once, he pressed the brittle bones against the glass. There was a snapping noise, and a long, yellow finger clattered to the floor.

'Ooh,' said Springy. 'You *fool*, Alker. Give it here!'

Perhaps worried about what he'd done, Alker decided to get rid. He looked about him for a place, then tossed the bunch of bones onto a table top. He bent swiftly and picked up the broken one. He threw that on the table, too.

'There you are,' he said. 'Stupid rotten things anyway. Boring.'

For Springy, that might have been the end of it. But Sam was wild with anger. She faced Alker on the platform, hardly able to control herself.

'You've broken it,' she said, through clenched teeth. 'You've smashed his hand.'

She made a grab at Alker, who tried to dodge. He wasn't quick enough. The boy and the girl struggled silently beside the pond.

After a few seconds, it was clear that Alker was winning. He was bigger and stronger than Sam.

Springy stood beside his sister, unsure what to do.

'Yah!' crowed Alker. 'You're just a soppy girl. I'll break your bones, too.'

Springy, who normally kept his temper, lost it then. He said to Sam: 'Let go!'

She did, immediately, as if she knew exactly what was in his mind. Alker, freed, stood beside the deep pool wondering what was going on.

Then, as if at a signal, the twins moved forward and shoved him in. It was easy.

Even before he hit the water, with a mighty splash, they realised that they'd been watched.

The door had opened, and their teacher was there.

Oh dear, thought Springy. The Rogues' Gallery.

Mrs Jackson had her evidence!

10 · Lies, Lies, Lies!

Sadly for Lapwing School, maybe, Peter Alker could swim and the biology pool, although deep, was not the Atlantic Ocean.

He made a noise, a terrific noise, and he made an awful mess. But before long, he was out, and he was raring for a fight.

'They pushed me!' he yelled. 'They tried to drown me! Call the police!'

As far as the twins could see, Mrs Jackson was trying hard not to burst out laughing.

'In a pig's patootie I will,' she said. 'Who says they pushed you? Sam? Springy? Is this true?'

They gaped, because they were both almost certain that she had seen them. They weren't stupid, either. It could be a trap. They said nothing.

Alker did, though. He ranted and roared and behaved appallingly. He kept shouting at Mrs Jackson, too. It was a big mistake.

'They'll have to go to the Head,' he yelled. 'And I'm going to ring up Mum and get her along! I want them expelled!'

'But Peter,' said Mrs Jackson, calmly. 'You know my rules. If somebody is accused of something and there is no proof, I don't punish them.'

'No proof! Look at my clothes! Look at me! I'm soaked to the skin!'

'You're wet, I'll admit,' said the teacher. 'If I can find in any way that the twins had a hand in that, they'll certainly be punished.'

'They pushed me! Both of them!'

Mrs Jackson turned to Springy and Sam.

'Well?'

Springy looked at Sam. Sam looked at Springy. Then she held up part of Captain Ahab.

'We went home and got his hands and foot, Miss. Then Alker stole a hand and broke a finger. There was a bit of a barney.'

'Golly goloon,' said Mrs Jackson. 'A bit of a barney, was there? Jostling, was there? Horseplay?'

'Yes,' said Alker. 'They – '

'You dry up,' she said. 'Oh, sorry, that wasn't meant to be a joke. Twins – do you admit it? Was there horseplay?'

They nodded. It was stupid to deny it. Mrs

Jackson nodded as well.

'Well,' she said. 'Evidence at last. All three of you agreed. There was horseplay.'

It was a trap, and Alker fell right into it.

'But *after* the horseplay, they pushed me in.'

'Oh no,' said the teacher. '*After* the horseplay I'm not interested in, Alker. The horseplay is the crime, and the horseplay is enough. You are all bad children who deserve throwing into a dungeon for six years and a week. Instead, you're going into the Rogues' Gallery. This afternoon.'

Alker shouted: 'But that's not fair! I want the Head! They almost drowned me!'

'Proof,' said Mrs Jackson. 'Evidence. Where is it?'

'I'm going home,' he said. He headed for the door.

Mrs Jackson lost her smile. She moved swiftly to the doorway and stood in front of him, so that he could not pass.

'Oh no you're not,' she said. 'We'll take you to the medical room and get a blanket. We'll dry your things out. *You're* being punished, Peter, not just the twins. Understand?'

Painting their portraits for the Rogues' Gallery was more like fun than punishment, when it came to it.

Especially as the class was told about the extra

skeleton bits to look at.

Especially as they were also told that Peter Alker had somehow ended up in the biology pool while fighting Springy and Sam.

Especially as he looked a proper drip, sitting in a corner wrapped in a big pink blanket.

Everybody wanted to talk to Springy and Sam, and congratulate them, and be their friends. Everyone except Beavham. And as Alker wouldn't speak to *him*, because he was sulking, Beavham went lonely.

Finally, the portraits were done. Springy and Sam took them to the front. Mrs Jackson looked at them, long and hard.

'Mm, not bad,' she said. 'Although you're both much uglier in real life. What are your criminal names to be?'

'Slippery Springy and Slimy Sam!' shouted someone. It was Damon. When everyone turned to stare he went bright pink.

'I knew they'd get up there soon,' he said. 'So I asked my Mum.'

Everybody laughed, but it was agreed. The names were stencilled on, and they joined Perilous Pete on the green cloth. A cheer went up.

'It's very serious really,' said Mrs Jackson. 'Although luckily the biology pool's all right, and the fish and so on don't even seem to have noticed the extra whale among them. But it is a punishment, remember. While you're in the gallery, you can't win stars.'

'Not even for Ahab's hands and foot?' asked Springy.

'Not even if the whole shebang danced in rattling its bones! What's more, I'm taking you home tonight. I want to talk about this skeleton, with your parents.'

For the first time that afternoon, Peter Alker cheered up.

One look at their faces was enough . . .

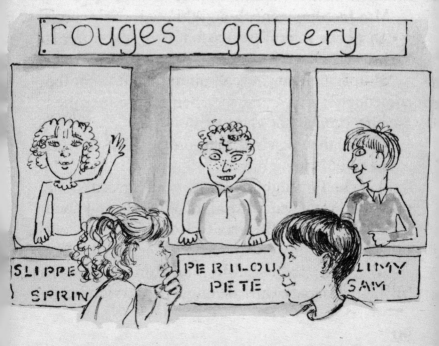

Mrs Jackson was well aware, as she drove them home, that the whole business with the skeleton was a very dicey one for them. Maybe that was their *real* punishment, they guessed, for tossing Alker into the pool.

She asked them, and they told her, the full story, about how Uncle Jock had beetled off at just the wrong moment, and about how they'd 'borrowed' the skeleton key.

'We haven't even put it back yet,' said Sam. 'Crikey, do you *have* to talk to Mum, Miss?'

'He said we could borrow Ahab,' added Springy. 'And it was your fault because you thought we were telling lies. It riled us up.'

Mrs Jackson went thoughtful.

'Yes,' she said. 'I suppose it could have done. Oh dear. There have been quite a few lies one way and another, haven't there? Especially this afternoon.'

They hoped she'd let them off, but they were almost home. Mrs Jackson sighed as she switched off the ignition.

'Maybe I'm doing the wrong thing,' she said. 'But I'd better see it through. What do you think they'll say, your Mum and Dad?'

Standing outside the front door, which Mrs Jackson said they should knock on, as she was there, not just walk through, they wondered.

Whatever it was, it would not be good. They'd cut too many corners this time. Far too many.

But when the door was opened from inside, they almost collapsed.

'Uncle Jock!' said Sam. 'You're *back*!'

Springy jumped on him, yelling, and the old fellow almost fell down.

'Crimes,' he said. 'What a welcome. I've only been gone two days!'

Mrs Jackson held a plastic bag out open. It contained the skull of Captain Ahab, and his hands and foot.

'You're Uncle Jock,' she said. 'I'm Mrs Jackson, a teacher. I believe these belong to an old friend of yours.'

Uncle Jock smiled, and shook her hand.

'Captain Ahab's,' he said. 'I've just been off trying to get a spare leg for him, down in Romsey, but I had no luck. You've come for the rest of him, I suppose?'

'Romsey?' said Sam. 'Why Romsey?'

'Shut up,' hissed Springy. 'Here comes Mum.'

'That would be nice, if you don't mind,' Mrs Jackson said to Uncle Jock. 'I've got the car outside.'

Mum was wiping her hands on a towel. She looked worried when she saw the teacher.

'Hallo,' she said. 'Stephen? Samantha? Have

you been up to something?'

'Not a bit of it,' said Uncle Jock. 'I gave the kids some bits of skeleton to take to school, that's all. They couldn't carry it all, so here's the teacher lady come along to cart him off.'

Mum was totally uninterested.

'Oh,' she said. 'Sam – offer Mrs Jackson a cup of tea.' Then she thought of something. 'Talking of skeletons, Uncle Jock,' she added. 'Whatever happened to that key you made me? I can't find it anywhere.'

Uncle Jock had guessed long ago. He winked at Springy.

'I'll knock you up another one tonight,' he said. 'How about ten minutes?'

'Smashing,' said Mum. 'And how are they doing at school, Mrs Jackson? Are they being good?'

Mrs Jackson threw back her head and laughed.

'Oh yes!' she said. 'They've got their pictures on the classroom wall already! No word of a lie.'

Springy and Sam darted through the door and raced up to the attic.

They left their mother looking rather pleased . . .

A Selected List of Fiction from Mammoth

While every effort is made to keep prices low, it is sometimes necessary to increase prices at short notice. Mammoth Books reserves the right to show new retail prices on covers which may differ from those previously advertised in the text or elsewhere.

The prices shown below were correct at the time of going to press.

☐	7497 0366 0	**Dilly the Dinosaur**	Tony Bradman £1.99
☐	7497 0021 1	**Dilly and the Tiger**	Tony Bradman £1.99
☐	7497 0137 4	**Flat Stanley**	Jeff Brown £1.99
☐	7497 0048 3	**Friends and Brothers**	Dick King-Smith £1.99
☐	7497 0054 8	**My Naughty Little Sister**	Dorothy Edwards £1.99
☐	416 86550 X	**Cat Who Wanted to go Home**	Jill Tomlinson £1.99
☐	7497 0166 8	**The Witch's Big Toe**	Ralph Wright £1.99
☐	7497 0218 4	**Lucy Jane at the Ballet**	Susan Hampshire £2.25
☐	416 03212 5	**I Don't Want To!**	Bel Mooney £1.99
☐	7497 0030 0	**I Can't Find It!**	Bel Mooney £1.99
☐	7497 0032 7	**The Bear Who Stood on His Head**	W. J. Corbett £1.99
☐	416 10362 6	**Owl and Billy**	Martin Waddell £1.75
☐	416 13822 5	**It's Abigail Again**	Moira Miller £1.75
☐	7497 0031 9	**King Tubbitum and the Little Cook**	Margaret Ryan £1.99
☐	7497 0041 6	**The Quiet Pirate**	Andrew Matthews £1.99
☐	7497 0064 5	**Grump and the Hairy Mammoth**	Derek Sampson £1.99

All these books are available at your bookshop or newsagent, or can be ordered direct from the publisher. Just tick the titles you want and fill in the form below.

Mandarin Paperbacks, Cash Sales Department, PO Box 11, Falmouth, Cornwall TR10 9EN.

Please send cheque or postal order, no currency, for purchase price quoted and allow the following for postage and packing:

UK	80p for the first book, 20p for each additional book ordered to a maximum charge of £2.00.
BFPO	80p for the first book, 20p for each additional book.
Overseas including Eire	£1.50 for the first book, £1.00 for the second and 30p for each additional book thereafter.

NAME (Block letters) ....

ADDRESS ....

....

....